The Secret Birthday Message

For Bill Martin

The Secret Birthday Message
By Eric Carle

HarperCollinsPublishers
 Printed in Hong Kong. Published in West Germany, 1971;
and in the United States of America, Canada, and the United Kingdom, 1972.

ISBN 0-690-72347-4.—ISBN 0-690-72348-2 (lib. bdg.)
LC Card 85-45403
17 18 19 20

On the night before Tim's birthday he found a strange envelope under his pillow. He sat up straight in his bed and opened the letter. Inside was a Secret Message!

And this is what it said:

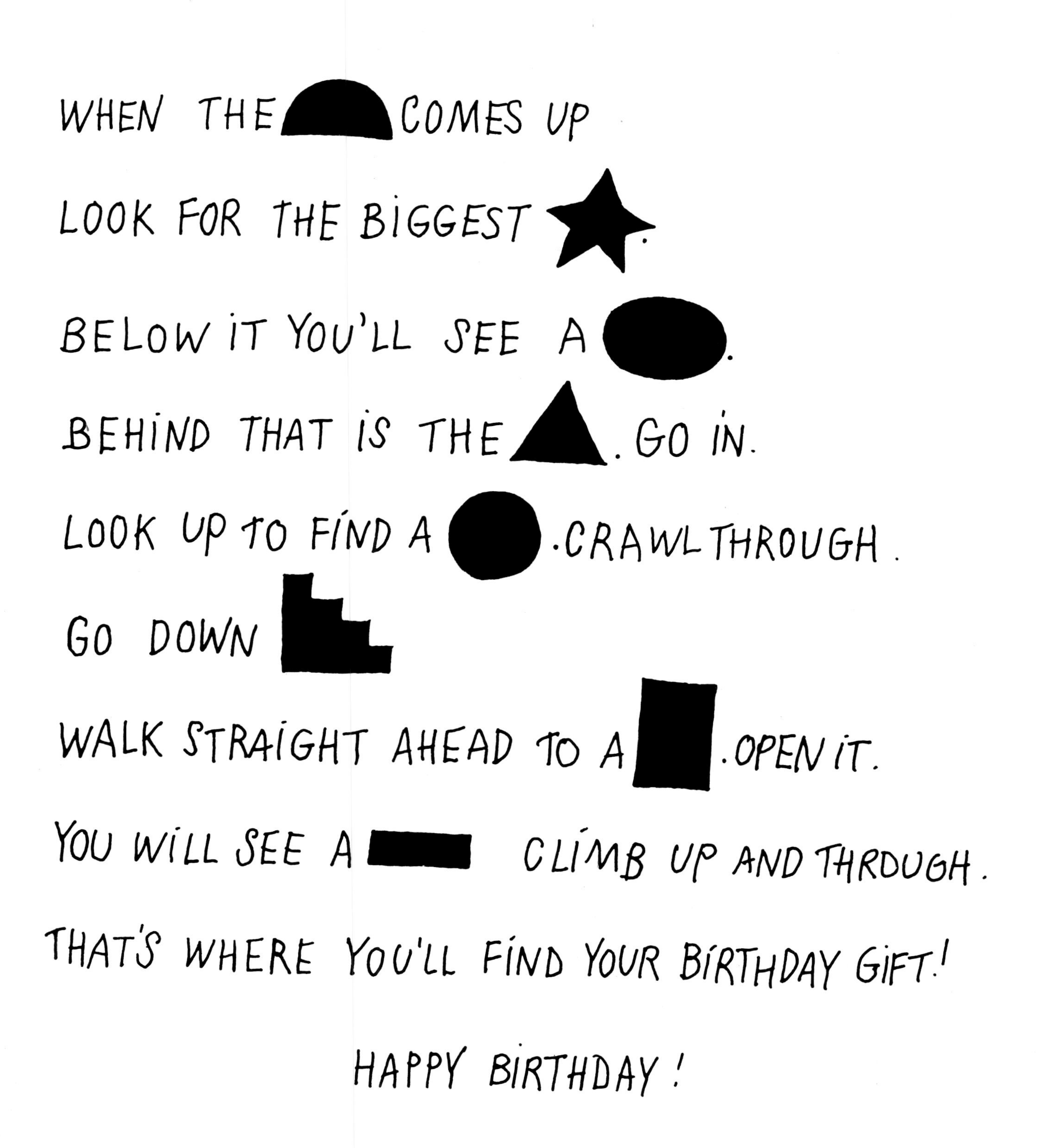
WHEN THE COMES UP
LOOK FOR THE BIGGEST .
BELOW IT YOU'LL SEE A .
BEHIND THAT IS THE . GO IN.
LOOK UP TO FIND A . CRAWL THROUGH.
GO DOWN
WALK STRAIGHT AHEAD TO A . OPEN IT.
YOU WILL SEE A CLIMB UP AND THROUGH.
THAT'S WHERE YOU'LL FIND YOUR BIRTHDAY GIFT!
HAPPY BIRTHDAY!

When the moon comes up

Look for the biggest star.

Below it you'll see a rock.

Look up to find a round opening. Crawl through.

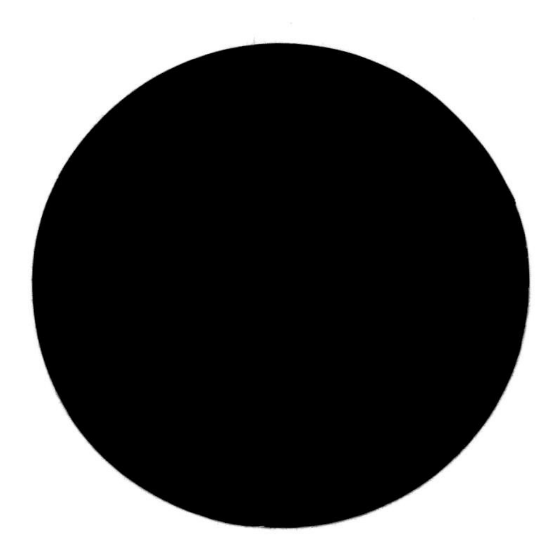

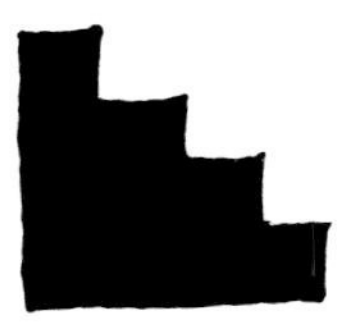

Go down the stairs.

HAPPY
BIRTHDAY

ERIC CARLE

ERIC CARLE, internationally known author and illustrator, believes that children really enjoy learning, and his award-winning picture books reflect this conviction. Filled with color and humor, each of his strikingly designed books brings the child a happy lesson in counting, or reading, or provides a pleasant introduction to the days of the week, the seasons, or other basic concepts.

Born in the United States, Mr. Carle spent his early years in Germany, and studied at the Akademie der bildenden Künste in Stuttgart. His books have been published in Japan, England, and many countries in Europe, as well as in the United States, and one of them was chosen the best picture book at the International Children's Book Fair in 1970. *Do You Want to Be My Friend?*, published in 1971, was an Honor Book in *Book World*'s Children's Spring Festival.